Anonymous

The Poets of the Elizabethan age

A selection of their most celebrated songs and sonnets

Anonymous

The Poets of the Elizabethan age
A selection of their most celebrated songs and sonnets

ISBN/EAN: 9783337175788

Printed in Europe, USA, Canada, Australia, Japan

Cover: Foto ©Andreas Hilbeck / pixelio.de

More available books at **www.hansebooks.com**

THE POETS

OF

THE ELIZABETHAN AGE.

A SELECTION OF

THEIR MOST CELEBRATED SONGS AND SONNETS.

Illustrated with Thirty Engravings.

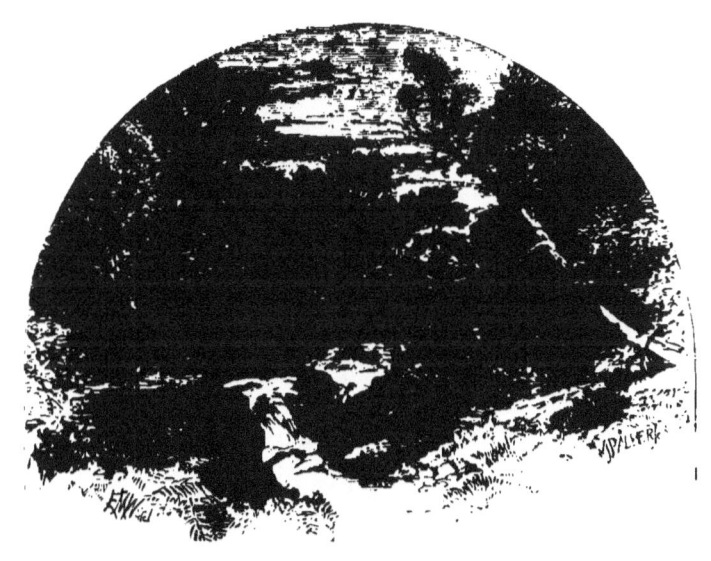

LONDON:

SAMPSON LOW, SON, & CO. 47, LUDGATE HILL.

1862.

R. Clay, Son, & Taylor, Printers, London.

CONTENTS.

——————

The Editor has included a few Poems which were written before the time of Elizabeth, and a few which properly belong to the early part of the reign of James the First. They all partake of a similar character, and stand unrivalled for the elegance of their language and their exquisite thought.

LIST OF ILLUSTRATIONS.

BLAME NOT MY LUTE.

BLAME not my Lute! for he must sound
  Of this or that as liketh me;
For lack of wit the Lute is bound
  To give such tunes as pleaseth me;
Though my songs be somewhat strange,
And speak such words as touch my change,
         Blame not my Lute!

My Lute, alas! doth not offend,
  Though that perforce he must agree
To sound such tunes as I intend,
  To sing to them that heareth me;
Then though my songs be somewhat plain,
And toucheth some that use to feign,
         Blame not my Lute!

          B

BLAME NOT MY LUTE.

My Lute and strings may not deny,
   But as I strike they must obey;
Break not them then so wrongfully,
   But wreak thyself some other way;
And though the songs which I indite,
Do quit thy change with rightful spite,
          Blame not my Lute!

Spite asketh spite, and changing change,
   And falsed faith, must needs be known;
The faults so great, the case so strange;
   Of right it must abroad be blown:
Then since that by thine own desert
My songs do tell how true thou art,
          Blame not my Lute!

Blame but thyself that hast misdone,
   And well deserved to have blame;
Change thou thy way, so evil begone,
   And then my Lute shall sound that same;
But if till then my fingers play,
By thy desert their wonted way,
          Blame not my Lute!

Farewell! unknown; for though thou break
   My strings in spite with great disdain,
Yet have I found out for thy sake,
   Strings for to string my Lute again:
And if perchance this silly rhyme,
Do make thee blush at any time,
          Blame not my Lute!

                SIR THOMAS WYAT.

SPRING.

The soote* season, that bud and bloom forth brings,
With green hath clad the hill and eke the vale:
The nightingale with feathers new she sings;
The turtle to her mate hath told her tale:

* Sweet.

Summer is come, for every spray now springs;
The hart hath hung his old head on the pale;
The buck in brake his winter coat he flings;
The fishes flete with new-repaired scale;
The adder all her slough away she slings;
The swift swallow pursueth the flies smale;
The busy bee her honey now she mings;
Winter is worn that was the flowers' bale:
And thus I see among these pleasant things
Each care decays, and yet my sorrow springs.

HENRY HOWARD, EARL OF SURREY.

COME, SLEEP, O SLEEP.

COME, Sleep, O Sleep, the certain knot of peace,
The baiting place of wit, the balm of woe,
The poor man's wealth, the prisoner's release,
The indifferent judge between the high and low.
With shield of proof shield me from out the prease
Of those fierce darts, Despair at me doth throw;
O make in me those civil wars to cease:
I will good tribute pay, if thou do so.
Take thou of me smooth pillows, sweetest bed;
A chamber, deaf to noise, and blind to light;

A rosy garland, and a weary head.
And if these things, as being thine by right,
Move not thy heavy grace, thou shalt in me
Livelier than elsewhere Stella's image see.

Having this day my horse, my hand my lance
Guided so well, that I obtain'd the prize,
Both by the judgment of the English eyes,
And of some sent from that sweet enemy France;
Horsemen my skill in horsemanship advance;
Townfolks my strength; a daintier judge applies
His praise to sleight which from good use doth rise;
Some lucky wits impute it but to chance;
Others, because of both sides I do take
My blood from them who did excel in this,
Think Nature me a man of arms did make.
How far they shot awry! the true cause is,
Stella look'd on, and from her heavenly face
Sent forth the beams which made so fair my race.

SIR PHILIP SIDNEY.

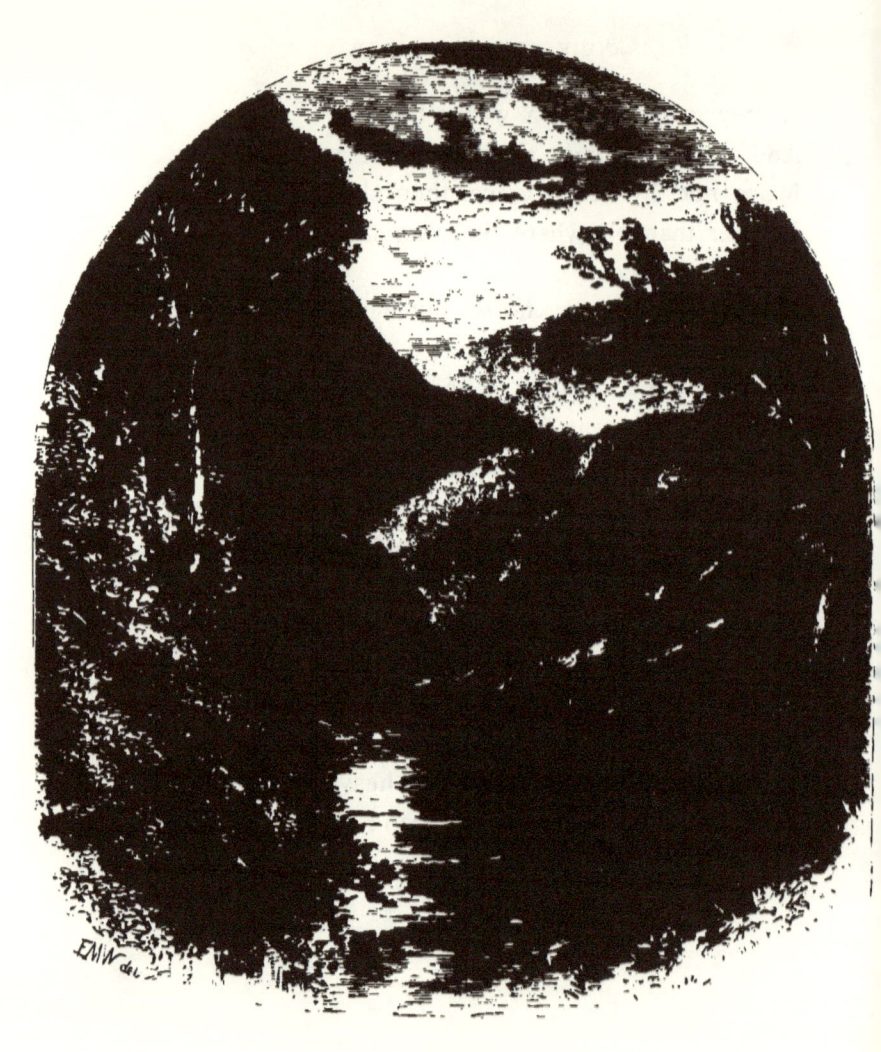

SONNET.

WITH how sad steps, O Moon! thou climb'st the skies,
How silently, and with how wan a face!
What may it be, that even in heavenly place
That busy Archer his sharp arrows tries?

14

SONNET.

Sure, if that long with love acquainted eyes
Can judge of love, thou feel'st a lover's case;
I read it in thy looks, thy languish'd grace
To me that feel the like thy state descries.
Then, even of fellowship, O Moon, tell me,
Is constant love deem'd there but want of wit?
Are beauties there as proud as here they be?
Do they above love to be lov'd, and yet
Those lovers scorn whom that love doth possess?
Do they call virtue there ungratefulness?

SIR PHILIP SIDNEY.

SONG.

HAVE I caught my heav'nly jewel,
    Teaching sleep most fair to be?
    Now will I teach her that she,
When she wakes, is too too cruel.

Since sweet sleep her eyes hath charm'd,
    The two only darts of Love;
    Now will I, with that boy, prove
Some play, while he is disarm'd.

15

Her tongue, waking, still refuseth,
    Giving frankly niggard *no:*
    Now will I attempt to know,
What *no* her tongue, sleeping, useth.

See the hand which, waking, guardeth,
    Sleeping, grants a free resort:
    Now will I invade the fort;
Cowards Love with loss rewardeth.

But, O fool! think of the danger
    Of her just and high disdain:
    Now will I, alas! refrain;
Love fears nothing else but anger.

Yet those lips, so sweetly swelling,
    Do invite a stealing kiss:
    Now will I but venture this,
Who will read, must first learn spelling.

O! sweet kiss! but ah! she's waking;
    Low'ring beauty chastens me:
    Now will I away hence flee:
Fool! more fool! for no more taking.

                 SIR PHILIP SIDNEY.

SAMELA.

Like to Diana in her summer weed,
Girt with a crimson robe of brightest dye,
　　　　Goes fair Samela;
Whiter than be the flocks that straggling feed,
When washed by Arethusa faint they lie,
　　　　Is fair Samela;
As fair Aurora in her morning grey,
Decked with the ruddy glister of her love,
　　　　Is fair Samela;
Like lovely Thetis on a calmèd day,
Whenas her brightness Neptune's fancy move,
　　　　Shines fair Samela;
Her tresses gold, her eyes like glassy streams,
Her teeth are pearl, the breasts are ivory
　　　　Of fair Samela;
Her cheeks, like rose and lily yield forth gleams,
Her brows' bright arches framed of ebony;
　　　　Thus fair Samela
Passeth fair Venus in her bravest hue,
And Juno in the show of majesty,
　　　　For she's Samela:
Pallas in wit, all three, if you will view,
For beauty, wit, and matchless dignity
　　　　Yield to Samela.

ROBERT GREENE.

C

CONTENT—A SONNET.

SWEET are the thoughts that savour of content :
The quiet mind is richer than a crown :
Sweet are the nights in careless slumber spent :
The poor estate scorns Fortune's angry frown.
Such sweet content, such minds, such sleep, such bliss,
Beggars enjoy, when princes oft do miss.
The homely house that harbours quiet rest,
The cottage that affords no pride nor care,
The mean, that 'grees with country music best,
The sweet consort of mirth's and music's fare.
Obscured life sets down a type of bliss ;
A mind content both crown and kingdom is.

ROBERT GREENE.

SONNET.

When May is in his prime and youthful spring
Doth clothe the tree with leaves, and ground with flowers,
And time of year reviveth every thing,
And lovely nature smiles, and nothing lours;

19

SONNET.

Then Philomela most doth strain her breast
With night-complaints, and sits in little rest.
This bird's estate may be compared with mine,
To whom fond love doth work such wrongs by day,
That in the night my heart must needs repine
And storm with sighs, to ease me as I may,
Whilst others are becalm'd, or lie them still,
Or sail secure, with tide and wind at will.
And as all those which hear this bird complain
Conceive in all her tunes a sweet delight,
Without remorse or pitying her pain ;
So she, for whom I wail both day and night,
Doth sport herself in hearing my complaint :
A just reward for serving such a saint.

THOMAS WATSON.

THE PASSIONATE SHEPHERD TO HIS LOVE.

COME live with me, and be my love,
And we will all the pleasures prove
That valleys, groves, and hills and fields,
Woods or steepy mountains yields.

And we will sit upon the rocks,
Seeing the shepherds feed their flocks,
By shallow rivers, to whose falls
Melodious birds sing madrigals.

And I will make thee beds of roses,
And a thousand fragrant posies ;
A cap of flowers and a kirtle,
Embroider'd all with leaves of myrtle :

A gown made of the finest wool,
Which from our pretty lambs we pull;
Fair lined slippers for the cold,
With buckles of the purest gold:

A belt of straw and ivy buds,
With coral clasps and amber studs;
And if these pleasures may thee move,
Come live with me, and be my love.

The shepherd swains shall dance and sing,
For thy delight, each May-morning:
If these delights thy mind may move,
Then live with me, and be my love.

KIT MARLOW.

LOVE'S SERVILE LOT.

LOVE, mistress is of many minds,
  Yet few know whom they serve;
They reckon least how little Love
  Their service doth deserve.

The will she robbeth from the wit,
  The sense from reason's lore;
She is delightful in the rind,
  Corrupted in the core.

She shroudeth vice in virtue's veil,
  Pretending good in ill;
She offereth joy, affordeth grief,
  A kiss where she doth kill.

A honey-shower rains from her lips,
  Sweet lights shine in her face;
She hath the blush of virgin mind,
  The mind of viper's race.

She makes thee seek, yet fear to find
  To find, but not enjoy:
In many frowns some gliding smiles
  She yields to more annoy.

She woos thee to come near her fire,
  Yet doth she draw it from thee;
Far off she makes thy heart to fry,
  And yet to freeze within thee.

She letteth fall some luring baits
  For fools to gather up;
Too sweet, too sour, to every taste
  She tempereth her cup.

Soft souls she binds in tender twist,
    Small flies in spinner's web ;
She sets afloat some luring streams,
    But makes them soon to ebb.

Her watery eyes have burning force ;
    Her floods and flames conspire :
Tears kindle sparks, sobs fuel are,
    And sighs do blow her fire.

May never was the month of love, .
    For May is full of flowers ;
But rather April, wet by kind,
    For love is full of showers.

Like tyrant, cruel wounds she gives,
    Like surgeon, salve she lends ;
But salve and sore have equal force,
    For death is both their ends.

With soothing words enthralled souls
    She chains in servile bands;
Her eye in silence hath a speech
    Which eye best understands.

Her little sweet hath many sours,
    Short hap immortal harms ;
Her loving looks are murd'ring darts,
    Her songs bewitching charms.

Like winter rose and summer ice,
  Her joys are still untimely;
Before her Hope, behind Remorse :
  Fair first, in fine unseemly.

Moods, passions, fancy's jealous fits
  Attend upon her train :
She yieldeth rest without repose,
  And heaven in hellish pain.

Her house is Sloth, her door Deceit,
  And slippery Hope her stairs ;
Unbashful Boldness bids her guests,
  And every vice repairs.

Her diet is of such delights
  As please till they be past ;
But then the poison kills the heart
  That did entice the taste.

Her sleep in sin doth end in wrath,
  Remorse rings her awake ;
Death calls her up, Shame drives her out,
  Despairs her upshot make.

Plough not the seas, sow not the sands,
  Leave off your idle pain ;
Seek other mistress for your minds,
  Love's service is in vain.

ROBERT SOUTHWELL.

CUPID AND CAMPASPE.

Cupid and my Campaspe played
At cards for kisses—Cupid paid;
He stakes his quiver, bow and arrows,
His mother's doves, and team of sparrows;
Loses them too, then down he throws
The coral of his lip, the rose
Growing on's cheek (but none knows how);
With these, the crystal of his brow,
And then the dimple of his chin;
All these did my Campaspe win.
At last he set her both his eyes;
She won, and Cupid blind did rise.
O Love! has she done this to thee?
What shall, alas! become of me?

JOHN LYLY

◆

SONNET.

LIKE as a ship, that through the ocean wide,
By conduct of some star, doth make her way,
Whenas a storm hath dimm'd her trusty guide,
Out of her course doth wander far astray;
So I, whose star, that wont with her bright ray
Me to direct, with clouds is overcast,
Do wander now, in darkness and dismay,
Through hidden perils round about me plast:

27

SONNET.

Yet hope I well that, when this storm is past,
My Helice, the lodestar of my life,
Will shine again, and look on me at last,
With lovely light to clear my cloudy grief.
Till then I wander careful, comfortless,
In secret sorrow, and sad pensiveness.

EDMUND SPENSER.

SONNET.

LIKE as the culver, on the bared bough,
Sits mourning for the absence of her mate,
And in her songs sends many a wishful vow
For his return, that seems to linger late :
So I alone, now left disconsolate,
Mourn to myself the absence of my love ;
And, wandering here and there all desolate,
Seek with my plaints to match that mournful dove :
Ne joy of ought that under heaven doth hove,
Can comfort me, but her own joyous sight ;
Whose sweet aspect both God and man can move,
In her unspotted pleasance to delight.
Dark is my day, whiles her fair light I miss,
And dead my life, that wants such lively bliss.

EDMUND SPENSER.

WHAT shepherd can express
The favour of her face?
To whom in this distress
I do appeal for grace;
 A thousand Cupids fly
 About her gentle eye;

From which each throws a dart
That kindleth soft sweet fire
Within my sighing heart;
Possessed by desire
 No sweeter life I try
 Than in her love to die.

The lily in the field
That glories in its white,
For pureness now must yield
And render up his right.
 Heaven pictur'd in her face
 Doth promise joy and grace.

Fair Cynthia's silver light
That beats on running streams,
Compares not with her white,
Whose hairs are all sunbeams.
 So bright my nymph doth shine
 As day unto my eyne.

With this there is a red,
Exceeds the damask rose:
Which in her cheeks is spread
Where every favour grows;
    In sky there is no star
    But she surmounts it far.

When Phœbus from the bed
Of Thetis doth arise,
The morning blushing red,
In fair carnation wise;
    He shows in my nymph's face,
    As queen of every grace.

This pleasant lily-white,
This taint of roseate red,
This Cynthia's silver light,
This sweet fair Dea spread,
    These sunbeams in mine eye,
    These beauties make me die.

                        EARL OF OXFORD.

WINTER.

FROM THE INDUCTION TO A MIRROUR FOR MAGISTRATES.

THE wrathful winter 'proching on apace,
With blust'ring blasts had all ybared the treen,
And old Saturnus with his frosty face
With chilling cold had pierced the tender green ;
The mantles rent, wherein enwrapped been
The gladsome groves that now lay overthrown,
The tapets torn, and every bloom down blown.

The soil that erst so seemly was to seen,
Was all despoil'd of her beauty's hue :
And soote fresh flowers (wherewith the summer's queen
Had clad the earth) now Boreas' blasts down blew,
And small fowls flocking, in their song did rue
The winter's wrath, wherewith each thing defaced
In woful wise bewailed the summer past.

31

Hawthorn had lost his motley livery,
The naked twigs were shivering all for cold;
And dropping down the tears abundantly;
Each thing (me thought) with weeping eye me told
The cruel season, bidding me withhold
My self within, for I was gotten out
Into the fields whereas I waiked about.

THOMAS SACKVILLE.

SONNET.

SOME glory in their birth, some in their skill,
Some in their wealth, some in their body's force;
Some in their garments, though new-fangled ill;
Some in their hawks and hounds, some in their horse;
And every humour hath its adjunct pleasure,
Wherein it finds a joy above the rest;
But these particulars are not my measure,
All these I better in one general best.
Thy love is better than high birth to me,
Richer than wealth, prouder than garments' cost,
Of more delight than hawks or horses be;
And having thee, of all men's pride I boast.
Wretched in this alone, that thou may'st take
All this away, and me most wretched make.

WILLIAM SHAKESPEARE.

THE PEDLAR'S SONG.

LAWN, as white as driven snow;
Cypress, black as e'er was crow;
Gloves, as sweet as damask roses;
Masks for faces, and for noses;
Bugle-bracelet, necklace-amber,
Perfume for a lady's chamber:
Golden quoifs and stomachers,
For my lads to give their dears;
Pins and poking-sticks of steel,
What maids lack from head to heel:
    Come, buy of me, come; come buy, come buy
    Buy, lads, or else your lasses cry.

WILLIAM SHAKESPEARE.

CRABBED AGE AND YOUTH.

CRABBED age and youth
  Cannot live together :
Youth is full of pleasance,
  Age is full of care ;
Youth like summer morn,
  Age like winter weather ;
Youth like summer brave,
  Age like winter bare.
Youth is full of sport,
Age's breath is short ;
  Youth is nimble, age is lame ;
Youth is hot and bold,
Age is weak and cold ;
  Youth is wild, and age is tame.
Age, I do abhor thee,
Youth, I do adore thee ;
  O, my love, my love is young !
Age, I do defy thee :—
O, sweet shepherd, hie thee !
  For methinks thou stay'st too long.

WILLIAM SHAKESPEARE.

JOG ON, JOG ON.

Jog on, jog on, the footpath way,
  And merrily hent the stile-a :
A merry heart goes all the day,
  Your sad tires in a mile-a.

WILLIAM SHAKESPEARE.

BLOW, BLOW, THOU WINTER WIND.

Blow, blow, thou winter wind,
Thou art not so unkind
    As man's ingratitude!
Thy tooth is not so keen,
Because thou art not seen,
    Although thy breath be rude.
Heigh, ho! sing heigh, ho! unto the green holly:
Most friendship is feigning, most loving mere folly.
    Then heigh, ho, the holly!
    This life is most jolly.

Freeze, freeze, thou bitter sky,
That dost not bite so nigh
    As benefits forgot!
Though thou the waters warp,
Thy sting is not so sharp
    As friend remember'd not.
    Heigh, ho! &c. &c.

WILLIAM SHAKESPEARE.

36

UNDER THE GREENWOOD TREE.

UNDER the greenwood tree,
Who loves to lie with me,
And tune his merry note
Unto the sweet bird's throat,
Come hither, come hither, come hither ;
    Here shall he see
    No enemy
But winter and rough weather.

Who doth ambition shun,
And loves to live i' the sun,
Seeking the food he eats,
And pleas'd with what he gets,
Come hither, come hither, come hither ;
    Here shall he see
    No enemy
But winter and rough weather.

WILLIAM SHAKESPEARE.

WHEN ICICLES HANG.

WHEN icicles hang by the wall,
    And Dick the shepherd blows his nail,
And Tom bears logs into the hall,
    And milk comes frozen home in pail;
When blood is nipt, and ways be foul,
Then nightly sings the staring owl,
Tu-whoo!
Tu-whit! tu-whoo! a merry note,
While greasy Joan doth keel the pot.

38

When all aloud the wind doth blow,
  And coughing drowns the parson's saw,
And birds sit brooding in the snow,
  And Marian's nose looks red and raw;
When roasted crabs hiss in the bowl,
Then nightly sings the staring owl,
Tu-whoo!
Tu-whit! tu-whoo! a merry note,
While greasy Joan doth keel the pot.

                 WILLIAM SHAKESPEARE.

THE NYMPH'S REPLY

TO THE PASSIONATE SHEPHERD.

If all the world and love were young,
And truth in every shepherd's tongue,
These pretty pleasures might me move
To live with thee, and be thy love.

Time drives the flocks from field to fold,
When rivers rage and rocks ·grow cold;
And Philomel becometh dumb,
The rest complain of cares to come.

The flowers do fade, and wanton fields
To wayward winter reckoning yields ;
A honey tongue—a heart of gall,
Is fancy's spring, but sorrow's fall.

Thy gowns, thy shoes, thy beds of roses,
Thy cap, thy kirtle, and thy posies,
Soon break, soon wither, soon forgotten,
In folly ripe, in reason rotten.

Thy belt of straw and ivy buds,
Thy coral clasps and amber studs ;
All these in me no means can move
To come to thee and be thy love.

But could youth last, and love still breed
Had joys no date, nor age no need,
Then these delights my mind might move
To live with thee and be thy love.

SIR WALTER RALEIGH.

THE LIE.

Go, soul, the body's guest,
    Upon a thankless errand!
Fear not to touch the best,
    The truth shall be thy warrant:
      Go, since I needs must die,
      And give the world the lie.

Go, tell the court it glows,
  And shines like rotten wood;
Go, tell the church it shows
  What's good, and doth no good:
    If church and court reply,
    Then give them both the lie.

Tell potentates, they live
  Acting by others' action,
Not loved unless they give,
  Not strong but by a faction:
    If potentates reply,
    Give potentates the lie.

Tell men of high condition
  That manage the estate,
Their purpose is ambition,
  Their practice only hate:
    And if they once reply,
    Then give them all the lie.

Tell them that brave it most,
  They beg for more by spending,
Who in their greatest cost,
  Seek nothing but commending.
    And if they make reply,
    Then give them all the lie.

Tell zeal it wants devotion,
  Tell love it is but lust,
Tell time it is but motion,
  Tell flesh it is but dust:

And wish them not reply,
For thou must give the lie.

Tell age it daily wasteth,
    Tell honour how it alters,
Tell beauty how she blasteth,
    Tell favour how it falters :
        And as they shall reply,
        Give every one the lie.

Tell wit how much it wrangles
    In tickle points of niceness :
Tell wisdom she entangles
    Herself in over-wiseness :
        And when they do reply,
        Straight give them both the lie.

Tell physic of her boldness,
    Tell skill it is pretension,
Tell charity of coldness,
    Tell law it is contention :
        And as they do reply,
        So give them still the lie.

Tell fortune of her blindness,
    Tell nature of decay,
Tell friendship of unkindness,
    Tell justice of delay :
        And if they will reply,
        Then give them all the lie.

Tell arts they have no soundness
  But vary by esteeming,
Tell schools they want profoundness,
  And stand too much on seeming :
    If arts and schools reply,
    Give arts and schools the lie.

Tell faith it's fled the city,
  Tell how the country erreth,
Tell, manhood shakes off pity,
  Tell, virtue least preferreth :
    And if they do reply,
    Spare not to give the lie.

So when thou hast, as I
  Commanded thee, done blabbing ·
Although to give the lie
  Deserves no less than stabbing ;
    Stab at thee he that will,
    No stab the soul can kill.

SIR WALTER RALEIGH.

SONNET.

Fair is my love, and cruel as she's fair ;
Her brow shades frown, although her eyes are sunny,
Her smiles are lightning, though her pride despair,
And her disdains are gall, her favours honey :
A modest maid, deck'd with a blush of honour,
Whose feet do tread green paths of youth and love ;
The wonder of all eyes that look upon her,
Sacred on earth, design'd a saint above.
Chastity and Beauty, which are deadly foes,
Live reconciled friends within her brow ;
And had she Pity to conjoin with those,
Then who had heard the plaints I utter now ?
For had she not been fair, and thus unkind,
My Muse had slept, and none had known my mind.

SAMUEL DANIEL.

BIRDS IN SPRING.

When Phœbus lifts his head out of the winter's wave,
No sooner doth the earth her flowery bosom brave,
At such time as the year brings on the pleasant spring,
But hunts-up to the morn the feath'red sylvans sing :
And in the lower grove, as on the rising knole,
Upon the highest spray of every mounting pole,

45

Those quiristers are perch't, with many a speckled breast,
Then from her burnisht gate the goodly glitt'ring east
Gilds every lofty top, which late the humorous night
Bespangled had with pearl, to please the morning's sight ;
On which the mirthful quires, with their clear open throats,

Unto the joyful morn so strain their warbling notes,
That hills and valleys ring, and even the echoing air
Seems all composed of sounds, about them everywhere.
The throstle, with shrill sharps, as purposely he song
T'awake the listless sun ; or chiding, that so long

He was in coming forth, that should the thickets thrill;
The ouzel near at hand, that hath a golden bill,
As nature had him markt of purpose, t' let us see
That from all other birds his tunes should different be;
For, with their vocal sounds, they sing to pleasant May;
Upon his dulcet pipe the merle doth only play.
When in the lower brake, the nightingale hard by,
In such lamenting strains the joyful hours doth ply,
As though the other birds she to her tunes would draw.
And, but that nature (by her all-constraining law)
Each bird to her own kind this season doth invite,
They else, alone to hear that charmer of the night,
(The more to use their ears,) their voices sure would spare,
That moduleth her tunes so admirably rare,
As man to set in parts at first had learn'd of her.

To Philomel the next, the linnet we prefer;
And by that warbling bird, the wood-lark place we then,
The red-sparrow, the nope, the red-breast, and the wren.
The yellow-pate; which though she hurt the blooming tree,
Yet scarce hath any bird a finer pipe than she.
And of these chaunting fowls, the goldfinch not behind,
That hath so many sorts descending from her kind.
The tydy for her notes as delicate as they,
The laughing hecco, then the counterfeiting jay,
The softer with the shrill (some hid among the leaves,
Some in the taller trees, some in the lower greaves)
Thus sing away the morn, until the mounting sun,
Through thick exhaled fogs his golden head hath run,
And through the twisted tops of our close covert creeps
To kiss the gentle shade, this while that sweetly sleeps.

MICHAEL DRAYTON.

VIRTUE.

SWEET day! so cool, so calm, so bright,
The bridal of the earth and sky;
The dews shall weep thy fall to-night;
    For thou must die.

Sweet rose! whose hue, angry and brave,
Bids the rash gazer wipe his eye;
Thy root is ever in its grave;
    And thou must die.

Sweet spring! full of sweet days and roses
A box where sweets compacted lie;
Thy music shows ye have your closes;
    And all must die.

Only a sweet and virtuous soul,
Like season'd timber never gives;
But, though the whole world turn to coal,
    Then chiefly lives.

GEORGE HERBERT.

SUNDAY.

O DAY most calm, most bright,
The fruit of this, the next world's bud,
The indorsement of supreme delight,
Writ by a Friend, and with His blood ;
The couch of time, care's balm and bay :
The week were dark, but for thy light ;
    Thy torch doth show the way.

The other days and thou
Make up one man; whose face *thou* art,
Knocking at heaven with thy brow:
The workydays are the back-part;
The burden of the week lies there,
Making the whole to stoop and bow,
    Till thy release appear.

    Man had straight forward gone
To endless death: but thou dost pull
And turn us round, to look on One,
Whom, if we were not very dull,
We could not choose but look on still;
Since there is no place so alone,
    The which He doth not fill.

    Sundays the pillars are,
On which heaven's palace arched lies:
The other days fill up the spare
And hollow room with vanities,
They are the fruitful beds and borders
In God's rich garden: that is bare,
    Which parts their ranks and orders.

    The Sundays of man's life,
Threaded together on Time's string,
Make bracelets to adorn the wife
Of the eternal glorious King.
On Sunday heaven's gate stands ope;
Blessings are plentiful and rife—
    More plentiful than hope.

SUNDAY.

This day my Saviour rose,
And did enclose this light for His;
That, as each beast his manger knows,
Man might not of his fodder miss.
Christ hath took in this piece of ground,
And made a garden there for those
    Who want herbs for their wound.

The rest of our creation
Our great Redeemer did remove
With the same shake, which at His passion
Did the earth and all the things move.
As Samson bore the doors away,
Christ's hands, though nail'd, wrought our salvation,
    And did unhinge that day.

The brightness of that day
We sullied by our foul offence:
Wherefore that robe we cast away
Having a new at His expense,
Whose drops of blood paid the full price,
That was required to make us gay,
    And fit for paradise.

Thou art a day of mirth:
And where the week-days trail on ground,
Thy flight is higher, as thy birth:
O let me take thee at the bound,
Leaping with thee from seven to seven,
Till that we both, being toss'd from earth,
    Fly hand in hand to heaven!

GEORGE HERBERT.

CELIA'S TRIUMPH.

SEE the chariot at hand here of love,
  Wherein my lady rideth!
Each that draws is a swan or a dove,
  And well the car Love guideth.
As she goes all hearts do duty
    Unto her beauty;
And enamour'd do wish, so they might
    But enjoy such a sight,
That they still were to run by her side,
Through swords, through seas, whither she would ride.

Do but look on her eyes, they do light
  All that love's world compriseth!
Do but look on her, she is bright
  As love's star when it riseth!
Do but mark, her forehead's smoother
    Than words that soothe her!

And from her arch'd brows, such a grace
　　Sheds itself through the face,
As alone there triumphs to the life
All the gain, all the good of the elements' strife.

Have you seen but a bright lily grow,
　Before rude hands have touch'd it ?
Have you mark'd but the fall of the snow,
　Before the soil hath smutch'd it ?
Have you felt the wool of the beaver,
　　Or swan's down ever ?
Or have smell'd of the bud o' the brier ?
　　Or the 'nard in the fire ?
Or have tasted the bag of the bee ?
O so white ! O so soft ! O so sweet is she !

BEN JONSON.

STILL TO BE NEAT.

STILL to be neat, still to be drest,
As you were going to a feast ;
Still to be powdered, still perfumed :
Lady, it is to be presumed,
Though art's hid causes are not found
All is not sweet, all is not sound.

Give me a look, give me a face,
That makes simplicity a grace ;

53

Robes loosely flowing, hair as free :
Such sweet neglect more taketh me,
Than all the adulteries of art ;
They strike mine eyes, but not my heart.

BEN JONSON.

TO THE QUEEN OF BOHEMIA.

You meaner beauties of the night,
  That poorly satisfy our eyes
More by your number than your light !

You common people of the skies!
What are you, when the sun shall rise?

You curious chanters of the wood
  That warble forth dame Nature's lays,
Thinking your voices understood
  By your weak accents! what's your praise
  When Philomel her voice shall raise?

You violets that first appear,
  By your pure purple mantles known,
Like the proud virgins of the year,
  As if the spring were all your own!
  What are you, when the rose is blown?

So, when my mistress shall be seen
  In form and beauty of her mind;
By virtue first, then choice, a Queen!
  Tell me, if she were not design'd
  Th' eclipse and glory of her kind?

SIR HENRY WOTTON.

SONG.

Why so pale and wan, fond lover?
    Prithee, why so pale?
Will, when looking well can't move her,
    Looking ill prevail?
    Prithee, why so pale?

Why so dull and mute, young sinner?
    Prithee, why so mute?
Will, when speaking well can't win her,
    Saying nothing do't?
    Prithee, why so mute?

Quit, quit for shame, this will not move,
    This cannot take her;
If of herself she will not love,
    Nothing can make her:
    The devil take her.

Sir John Suckling.

I LOVE (and have some cause to love) the earth :
She is my Maker's creature ; therefore good :
She is my mother, for she gave me birth ;
She is my tender nurse—she gives me food ;
    But what's a creature, Lord, compared with Thee ?
    Or what's my mother, or my nurse to me ?

I love the air : her dainty sweets refresh
My drooping soul, and to new sweets invite me ;
Her shrill-mouth'd quire sustains me with their flesh,
And with their polyphonian notes delight me :
    But what's the air or all the sweets that she
    Can bless my soul withal, compared with Thee ?

I love the sea : she is my fellow-creature,
My careful purveyor ; she provides me store :
She walls me round ; she makes my diet greater :
She wafts my treasure from a foreign shore :
    But, Lord of oceans, when compared with Thee,
    What is the ocean or her wealth to me ?

To heaven's high city I direct my journey,
Whose spangled suburbs entertain mine eye ;
Mine eye, by contemplation's great attorney,
Transcends the crystal pavements of the sky :
    But what is heaven, great God, compared to Thee ?
    Without Thy presence heaven's no heaven to me.

Without Thy presence earth gives no refection;
Without Thy presence sea affords no treasure;
Without Thy presence air's a rank infection;
Without Thy presence heaven itself no pleasure:
   If not possess'd, if not enjoy'd in Thee,
   What's earth, or sea, or air, or heaven to me?

The highest honours that the world can boast,
Are subjects far too low for my desire;
The brightest beams of glory are (at most)
But dying sparkles of Thy living fire:
   The loudest flames that earth can kindle, be
   But nightly glow-worms, if compared to Thee.

Without Thy presence wealth is bags of cares;
Wisdom but folly; joy disquiet—sadness:
Friendship is treason, and delights are snares!
Pleasure but pain, and mirth but pleasing madness;
   Without Thee, Lord, things be not what they be,
   Nor have they being, when compared with Thee.

In having all things, and not Thee, what have I?
Not having Thee, what have my labours got?
Let me enjoy but Thee, what further crave I?
And having Thee alone, what have I not?
   I wish nor sea nor land; nor would I be
   Possess'd of heaven, heaven unpossess'd of Thee.

FRANCIS QUARLES.

TO A NIGHTINGALE.

SWEET bird! that sing'st away the early hours
Of winters past, or coming, void of care.
Well pleased with delights which present are,
Fair seasons, budding sprays, sweet-smelling flowers :
To rocks, to springs, to rills, from leafy bowers,
Thou thy Creator's goodness dost declare,
And what dear gifts on thee He did not spare,
A stain to human sense in sin that low'rs.
What soul can be so sick which by thy songs
(Attir'd in sweetness) sweetly is not driven
Quite to forget earth's turmoils, spites, and wrongs,
And lift a reverend eye and thought to heaven ?
Sweet artless songster! thou my mind dost raise
To airs of spheres—yes, and to angels' lays.

WILLIAM DRUMMOND.

THE PRAISE OF A SOLITARY LIFE.

THRICE happy he who by some shady grove,
Far from the clamorous world, doth live his own.
Thou solitary, who is not alone,
But doth converse with that eternal love.
O how more sweet is bird's harmonious moan,
Or the hoarse sobbings of the widow'd dove,
Than those smooth whisperings near a prince's throne,
Which good make doubtful, do the evil approve!
O how more sweet is Zephyr's wholesome breath,
And sighs embalm'd which new-born flowers unfold,
Than that applause vain honour doth bequeath!
How sweet are streams to poison drank in gold!
The world is full of horror, troubles, slights:
Woods' harmless shades have only true delights.

WILLIAM DRUMMOND.

HAPPINESS OF THE SHEPHERD'S LIFE.

THRICE, oh thrice happy, shepherd's life and state!
When courts are happiness' unhappy pawns!
His cottage low and safely humble gate
Shuts out proud Fortune with her scorns and fawns:
No feared treason breaks his quiet sleep,
Singing all day, his flocks he learns to keep;
Himself as innocent as are the innocent sheep.

No Syrian worms he knows, that with their thread
Draw out their silken lives : nor silken pride :
His lambs' warm fleece well fits his little need,
Not in that proud Sidonian tincture dyed :
No empty hopes, no courtly fears him fright ;
Nor begging wants his middle fortune bite ;
But sweet content exiles both misery and spite.

Instead of music, and base flattering tongues,
Which wait to first salute my lord's uprise ;
The cheerful lark wakes him with early songs,
And birds sweet whistling notes unlock his eyes :
In country plays is all the strife he uses ;
Or sing, or dance unto the rural Muses ;
And but in music's sports all difference refuses.

His certain life, that never can deceive him,
Is full of thousand sweets, and rich content :
The smooth-leaved beeches in the field receive him
With coolest shades, till noon-tide rage is spent ;
His life is neither toss'd in boist'rous seas
Of troublous world, nor lost in slothful ease :
Pleas'd and full blest he lives, when he his God can please.

His bed of wool yields safe and quiet sleeps,
While by his side his faithful spouse hath place ;
His little son into his bosom creeps,
The lively picture of his father's face :
Never his humble house nor state torment him :
Less he could like, if less his God had sent him ;
And when he dies, green turfs, with grassy tomb, content him.

PHINEAS FLETCHER.

TO DAFFODILS.

FAIR daffodils, we weep to see
You haste away so soon ;
As yet the early-rising sun
Has not attain'd his noon :
      Stay, stay,
   Until the hast'ning day
       Has run
  But to the even-song ;
And having pray'd together, we
   Will go with you along !

We have short time to stay as you,
We have as short a spring ;
As quick a growth to meet decay,

63

As you or anything :
    We die,
As your hours do ; and dry
    Away
Like to the summer's rain,
Or as the pearls of morning dew
Ne'er to be found again.

ROBERT HERRICK.

A COUNTRY LIFE.

SWEET country life, to such unknown,
Whose lives are others', not their own !
But, serving courts and cities, be
Less happy, less enjoying thee.
Thou never plough'd the ocean's foam,
To seek and bring rough pepper home ;
Nor to the eastern Ind dost rove,
To bring from thence the scorched clove ;
Nor, with the loss of thy lov'd rest,
Bring'st home the ingot from the west.
No ; thy ambition's master-piece
Flies no thought higher than a fleece ;

Or how to pay thy hinds, and clear
All scores, and so to end the year ;
But walk'st about thy own dear grounds,

Not craving others' larger bounds ;
For well thou know'st 'tis not th' extent
Of land makes life, but sweet content.

When now the cock, the ploughman's horn,
Calls for the lily-wristed morn,
Then to thy corn-fields thou dost go,
Which, though well soil'd, yet thou dost know
That the best compost for the lands
Is the wise master's feet and hands.
There, at the plough, thou find'st thy team,
With a hind whistling there to them ;
And cheer'st them up by singing how
The kingdom's portion is the plough.
This done, then to th' enamelled meads
Thou go'st ; and, as thy foot there treads,
Thou seest a present god-like power
Imprinted in each herb and flower ;
And smell'st the breath of great-eyed kine,
Sweet as the blossoms of the vine.
Here thou behold'st thy large, sleek neat,
Unto the dewlaps up in meat ;
And, as thou look'st, the wanton steer,
The heifer, cow, and ox, draw near,
To make a pleasing pastime there.
These seen, thou go'st to view thy flocks
Of sheep, safe from the wolf and fox ;
And find'st their bellies there as full
Of short sweet grass, as backs with wool ;
And leav'st them, as they feed and fill,
A shepherd piping on the hill.

For sports, for pageantry, and plays,
Thou hast thy eves and holy-days,
On which the young men and maids meet
To exercise their dancing feet ;
Tripping the comely country round,

With daffodils and daisies crowned.
Thy wakes, thy quintels, here thou hast,
Thy May-poles, too, with garlands graced ;
Thy morris-dance, thy Whitsun ale,
Thy shearing feast, which never fail ;

A COUNTRY LIFE.

Thy harvest-home, thy wassail-bowl,
That's tost up after fox i' th' hole;
Thy mummeries, thy twelfth-night kings
And queens, and Christmas revellings;
Thy nut-brown mirth, thy russet wit,
And no man pays too dear for it.
To these thou hast thy time to go,
And trace the hare in the treacherous snow:
Thy witty wiles to draw, and get
The lark into the trammel net;
Thou hast thy cock rood, and thy glade,
To take the precious pheasant made!
Thy lime-twigs, snares, and pitfalls, then,
To catch the pilfering birds, not men.
O happy life, if that their good
The husbandmen but understood!
Who all the day themselves do please,
And younglings, with such sports as these;
And, lying down, have nought t' affright
Sweet sleep, that makes more short the night.

ROBERT HERRICK

DEATH'S FINAL CONQUEST.

THE glories of our birth and state
  Are shadows, not substantial things;
There is no armour against fate:
  Death lays his icy hands on kings;
      Sceptre and crown
      Must tumble down,
And in the dust be equal made
With the poor crooked scythe and spade.

Some men with swords may reap the field,
  And plant fresh laurels where they kill;
But their strong nerves at last must yield,
  They tame but one another still;
      Early or late,
      They stoop to fate,
And must give up their murmuring breath,
When they, pale captives, creep to death.

The garlands wither on your brow,
  Then boast no more your mighty deeds;
Upon Death's purple altar, now,
  See where the victor victim bleeds:
      All heads must come
      To the cold tomb,
Only the actions of the just
Smell sweet and blossom in the dust.

JAMES SHIRLEY.

SONNET UPON A STOLEN KISS.

Now gentle sleep hath closed up those eyes
Which, waking, kept my boldest thoughts in awe ;
And free access unto that sweet lip lies,
From whence I long the rosy breath to draw.
Methinks no wrong it were, if I should steal
From those two melting rubies, one poor kiss ;
None sees the theft that would the theft reveal,
Nor rob I her of ought what she can miss :
Nay should I twenty kisses take away,
There would be little sign I would do so ;
Why then should I this robbery delay ?
Oh ! she may wake, and therewith angry grow.
Well, if she do, I'll back restore that one,
And twenty hundred thousand more for loan.

GEORGE WITHER.

CHRISTMAS.

So now is come our joyful'st feast ;
　　Let every man be jolly ;
Each room with ivy leaves is drest,
　　And every post with holly.
Though some churls at our mirth repine,
Round your foreheads garlands twine,
Drown sorrow in a cup of wine,
　　And let us all be merry.

Now all our neighbours' chimneys smoke,
　　And Christmas blocks are burning ;
Their ovens they with baked meat choke,
　　And all their spits are turning.
Without the door let sorrow lie ;
And if for cold it hap to die,
We'll bury 't in a Christmas pie,
　　And evermore be merry.

Now every lad is wond'rous trim,
    And no man minds his labour ;
Our lasses have provided them
    A bagpipe and a tabor ;
Young men and maids, and girls and boys,
Give 'life to one another's joys ;
And you anon shall by their noise
    Perceive that they are merry.

Rank misers now do sparing shun ;
    Their hall of music soundeth ;
And dogs thence with whole shoulders run,
    So all things there aboundeth.
The country folks themselves advance,
With crowdy-muttons out of France ;
And Jack shall pipe and Gill shall dance,
    And all the town be merry.

Ned Squash hath fetcht his bands from pawn,
    And all his best apparel ;
Brisk Nell hath bought a ruff of lawn
    With dropping of the barrel.
And those that hardly all the year
Had bread to eat, or rags to wear,
Will have both clothes and dainty fare,
    And all the day be merry.

Now poor men to the justices
    With capons make their errants ;
And if they hap to fail of these,
    They plague them with their warrants :

But now they feed them with good cheer,
And what they want they take in beer,
For Christmas comes but once a year,
   And then they shall be merry.

Good farmers in the country nurse
   The poor, that else were undone ;
Some landlords spend their money worse,
   On lust and pride at London.
There the roysters they do play,
Drab and dice their lands away,
Which may be ours another day,
   And therefore let's be merry.

The client now his suit forbears,
   The prisoner's heart is eased ;
The debtor drinks away his cares,
   And for the time is pleased.
Though others' purses be more fat,
Why should we pine, or grieve at that ?
Hang sorrow ! care will kill a cat,
   And therefore let's be merry.

Hark ! now the wags abroad do call
   Each other forth to rambling ;
Anon you'll see them in the hall,
   For nuts and apples scrambling.
Hark ! how the roofs with laughter sound,
Anon they'll think the house goes round,
For they, the cellar's depth have found,
   And there they will be merry.

The wenches with their wassail bowls
   About the streets are singing;
The boys are come to catch the owls,
   The wild mare in is bringing.
Our kitchen boy hath broke his box,
And to the dealing of the ox,
Our honest neighbours come by flocks,
   And here they will be merry.

Now kings and queens poor sheepcotes have,
    And mate with every body;
The honest men now play the knave,
    And wise men play the noddy.
Some youths will now a mumming go,
Some others play at Roland-bo,
And twenty other game boys mo,
    Because they will be merry.

Then, wherefore, in these merry days,
    Should we, I pray, be duller?
No, let us sing some roundelays,
    To make our mirth the fuller:
And while we thus inspired sing,
Let all the streets with echoes ring;
Woods and hills, and everything,
    Bear witness we are merry.

GEORGE WITHER.

SONG.

THE lark now leaves his watery nest,
   And climbing shakes his dewy wings;
He takes his window for the east,
   And to implore your light, he sings,
Awake, awake, the moon will never rise,
Till she can dress her beauty at your eyes.

The merchant bows unto the seaman's star,
   The ploughman from the sun his season takes;
But still the lover wonders what they are,
   Who look for day before his mistress wakes:
Awake, awake, break through your veils of lawn!
Then draw your curtains and begin the dawn.

SIR WILLIAM DAVENANT.

THE ANGLER'S WISH.

I IN these flowery meads would be ;
These crystal streams should solace me ;
To whose harmonious bubbling noise,
I with my angle would rejoice ;
   Sit here and see the turtle-dove
   Court his chaste mate to acts of love ;

Or on that bank feel the west wind
Breathe health and plenty : please my mind.
To see sweet dew-drops kiss these flowers,
And then wash'd off by April showers ;
   Here, hear my Kenna sing a song ;
   There, see a blackbird feed her young,

Or a laverock build her nest:
Here, give my weary spirits rest,
And raise my low-pitched thoughts above
Earth, or what poor mortals love :
    Thus, free from law-suits and the noise
    Of princes' courts, I would rejoice.

Or, with my Bryan and a book,
Loiter long days near Shawford brook ;
There sit by him, and eat my meat,
There see the sun both rise and set,
There bid good morning to next day,
There 'meditate my time away,
    And angle on ; and beg to have
    A quiet passage to a welcome grave.

IZAAK WALTON.

GO, LOVELY ROSE—A SONG.

Go, lovely rose!
Tell her that wastes her time and me
That now she knows,
When I resemble her to thee,
How sweet and fair she seems to me.

Tell her, that's young,
And shuns to have her graces spied,
That, had'st thou sprung
In deserts, where no men abide,
Thou must have uncommended died.

Small is the worth
Of beauty from the light retir'd ;
Bid her come forth,
Suffer herself to be desir'd,
And not blush so to be admir'd.

Then die ! that she
The common fate of all things rare
May read in thee,
How small a part of time they share
That are so wondrous sweet and fair !

EDMUND WALLER.

WHEN first thy eyes unveil, give thy soul leave
To do the like ; our bodies but forerun
The spirit's duty : true hearts spread and leave
Unto their God, as flowers do to the sun :
Give Him thy first thoughts then, so shalt thou keep
Him company all day, and in Him sleep.
Yet never sleep the sun up ; prayer should
Dawn with the day : there are set awful hours
'Twixt heaven and us ; the manna was not good
After sun-rising ; far day sullies flowers :
Rise to prevent the sun ; sleep doth sins glut,
And heaven's gate opens when the world's is shut.
Walk with thy fellow creatures ; note the hush
And whisperings amongst them. Not a spring
Or leaf but hath his morning hymn ; each bush
And oak doth know I AM. Canst thou not sing ?
O leave thy cares and follies ! Go this way,
And thou art sure to prosper all the day.
Serve God before the world ; let Him not go
Until thou hast a blessing ; then resign
The whole unto Him, and remember who
Prevail'd by wrestling ere the sun did shine ;
Pour oil upon the stones, weep for thy sin,
Then journey on, and have an eye to heav'n.
Mornings are mysteries ; the first, the world's youth,
Man's resurrection, and the future's bud,

Shroud in their births; the crown of life, light, truth,
Is styled their star; the stone and hidden food:
Three blessings wait upon them, one of which
Should move—they make us holy, happy, rich.
When the world's up, and every swarm abroad,
Keep well thy temper, mix not with each clay;
Despatch necessities; life hath a load
Which must be carried on, and safely may;
Yet keep those cares without thee; let the heart
Be God's alone, and choose the better part.

VAUGHAN.

MY MIND TO ME A KINGDOM IS.

My mind to me a kingdom is,
  Such perfect joy therein I find,
That it excels all other bliss
  That God or Nature hath assign'd:
Though much I want that most would have,
Yet still my mind forbids to crave.

No princely port, or wealthy store,
  Nor force to win a victory;
No wily wit to salve a sore,
  No shape to win a loving eye;
To none of these I yield as thrall,
For why, my mind despise them all.

I see that plenty surfeits oft,
  And hasty climbers soonest fall;
I see that such as are aloft,
  Mishap doth threaten most of all;
These get with toil, and keep with fear:
Such cares my mind can never bear.

I press to bear no haughty sway;
  I wish no more than may suffice;
I do no more than well I may,
  Look what I want, my mind supplies;
Lo, thus I triumph like a king,
My mind's content with anything.

83

MY MIND TO ME A KINGDOM IS.

I laugh not at another's loss,
    Nor grudge not at another's gain ;
No worldly waves my mind can toss ;
    I brook that is another's bane ;
I fear no foe, nor fawn on friend ;
I loathe not life, nor dread mine end.

My wealth is health and perfect ease,
    And conscience clear my chief defence ;
I never seek by bribes to please,
    Nor by desert to give offence ;
Thus do I live, thus will I die ;
Would all do so as well as I !

ANONYMOUS.

R. Clay, Son, & Taylor, Printers, London.

www.ingramcontent.com/pod-product-compliance
Lightning Source LLC
Chambersburg PA
CBHW020757020726
47495CB00008B/2478